EMILY**RODDA**

Something Special

Illustrated by Noela Young

Angus&Robertson
An imprint of HarperCollins*Children'sBooks*

Angus&Robertson
An imprint of HarperCollins *Children's Books*, Australia

First published in Australia in 1984
This edition published in 2017
by HarperCollins *Publishers* Australia Pty Limited
ABN 36 009 913 517
harpercollins.com.au

HarperCollins *Publishers*
Level 13, 201 Elizabeth Street, Sydney NSW 2000, Australia
Unit D1, 63 Apollo Drive, Rosedale, Auckland 0632, New Zealand
A 53, Sector 57, Noida, UP, India
1 London Bridge Street, London SW1 9GF, United Kingdom
2 Bloor Street East, 20th floor, Toronto, Ontario M4W 1A8, Canada
195 Broadway, New York NY 10007, USA

A CiP record for this title is available from the National Library of Australia

ISBN 978 1 4607 5373 6 (pbk)
ISBN 978 1 4607 0824 8 (ebook)

Cover and internal illustrations by Noela Young
Cover design by Hazel Lam, HarperCollins Design Studio
Typeset in Sabon LT Std by Kelli Lonergan
Printed and bound in Australia by McPherson's Printing Group
The papers used by HarperCollins in the manufacture of this book are a
natural, recyclable product made from wood grown in sustainable plantation
forests. The fibre source and manufacturing processes meet recognised
international environmental standards, and carry certification.

For Kate, who read it first.

Contents

1. Getting Ready

The clothes kept coming. The fete was on Saturday, and the clothes kept coming.

'Nan said here's some more,' muttered Tiny Da Costa, staggering under the weight of a huge cardboard box.

'And Mum says this is the best she can do,' piped Cecilia Strong, pale under her freckles, muscles bulging under her tatty T-shirt.

'Get out of the way!' bawled Whitey McGoo. 'I'm coming through!'

There was a sickening thump.

'LIZZIE!' roared Sam's dad. 'Get in here! The place has gone mad!'

The clothes lay in heaps, the boxes teetered one on top of the other in the spare room, the room with the stained-glass window. The late afternoon sun shone through the glass bluebird, the milky sea, in thick, dusty beams. Sam moved through the box-maze. The room was very still.

Tomorrow her mother would finish sorting the clothes. By Saturday they'd be ready to be taken to the fete and put on racks and tables, to be sold. Second-hand clothes, marked with prices in her mother's curly writing. The boxes and bags bulged; the heaps of clothes lay lumpy and tumbling, legs and arms tangling.

There was a scuffle at the door. It was Toby. Their mother's footsteps pounded down the hall. Toby put his head down and crawled at top speed into the room, his bobbing bare bottom disappearing behind the first pile of boxes as Lizzie, dishevelled, appeared.

'Come back, you little devil,' shouted Lizzie. 'Oh, I'll give you such a thrashing!' A triumphant crow taunted her from the box-maze. Sam laughed. The chase began, and the sunbeams went wild as the dust flew.

'Bye, Sam, see you tomorrow.'

'See ya tomorrow ...'

'See ya ...'

The big red sign flapped on the school fence.

'And, honestly, it's been such a *business*!'

Sam's mother was saying to Mrs McGoo. 'The stuff some people have sent — just packed any old way. I don't even know who gave half of it. And all the stuff left over from last year! But there are some really beautiful things, too. A red satin evening dress that's just ...'

'C'mon, Mum,' whinged Sam. 'I'm thirsty.'

'Sam, I'm talking to Mrs McGoo. Just a minute. But,

Alice, you've never seen anything like the rubbish. One box had these hideous luminous *purple* fluffy slippers — all matted and ...'

'Oh, yes,' said Mrs McGoo, rather stiffly. 'I sent those. Of course, they're not to everyone's ...'

Sam's scalp prickled all over.

'Oh!' shrieked Lizzie. 'Oh, of course they'll *sell* like mad — they look terribly cosy. And lots of people love ... purple. Heavens, look at the time. Come on, Sam, we'd better rush. Goodbye, Alice. See you tomorrow.'

Sam and her mother rushed for the car. Lizzie was very pink. She clambered into the driver's seat and Sam slid into the back. They slammed their doors.

'Oh, Sam,' said Lizzie. 'Wasn't that *awful*.'

Dad and Toby were sitting on the front steps waiting for them. This usually meant that Toby hadn't been an angel, and that Dad's first words would be ...

'About time!' roared Dad. 'Hello, Sammy darling. Nice to have Mum picking you up today? Lizzie, this monster has been driving me ...'

'Sorry, darling, sorry. Anyway, we're here at last. You've no idea the awful thing that ...'

'He climbed onto the red chair and fell off and got a terrible crack on the head. He ate a piece of possum pooh. I tried to wash his mouth out and he ...'

They climbed the stairs, talking flat out. Toby, slung over Lizzie's shoulder, waved hello to Sam as they opened the door and the cool shade of home took them in.

2. The Spare Room

Now the best of the clothes hung on racks. They stirred as Sam walked between the rows, brushing a velvety sleeve, feeling a piece of lace, touching a button.

'They look good, don't they?' said Lizzie from the door.

'Is everything done now?' Sam asked anxiously.

'Absolutely done, worry-pot,' said Lizzie. 'Especially me!'

Sam looked at her mother. 'How are we going to get it all to school?'

'Don't worry, Sammy,' said Lizzie. 'It's all organised. I may be the only woman in the world who'd have to take two days off work to organise a fete stall, but at least it's done.'

She came into the room and started picking up bits of string and fluff from the floor. 'Do you want a piece of cheese, darling?'

'No thanks. Mum —'

'Yees …'

'Who gave us the red dress?'

'I don't know who sent anything any more. It's lovely, isn't it? I think it must have been a Special.'

'What's a Special?' asked Sam.

'Well, it's always seemed to me,' said Lizzie, 'that most clothes you wear are just clothes. You know. But every now and then you get something that you feel so good in, that suits you so well that —'

'It's a Special.'

'Yes. And somehow or other, when people think about you, they often think about you wearing that thing. It's funny.'

'Like Spotty, Mum? Is Spotty a Special?'

'Yeah, I suppose she is. Dear old Spotty,' said Lizzie. 'She's ancient now, but she's still all right, really, isn't she?' Thoughtfully she threaded a finger through two holes in Spotty's skirt.

There was a thump from the direction of the lounge room. Toby's voice rose in a surprised squeak. Then there was silence.

'Oh, gosh, that sounds bad. What's the little devil …' Lizzie darted out the door. Sam waited.

'Naughty boy touch Mummy's plant! Poor plant, all broken! Poor sore plant …' she heard.

'Adadoolah,' piped Toby's voice sympathetically.

Sam giggled to herself. She shut the door of the room and settled down in the big old chair in the comer, to enjoy the quiet.

3. Dreaming

It was very peaceful. The sun had reached the bird window now, and heavy beams began to push through the still air. The clothes seemed to move as the light played on their folds or streamed past, leaving them in the gloom. The dust motes whirled, glittering in the beams.

Sam blinked. The dust seemed to be getting into her eyes, dazzling and itching. Her head seemed full of voices, high and low, chattering, laughing …singing …singing …

'Daisy, Daisy, give me your answer, do!'

There was a lady in the comer. She was wearing the red satin dress. She was smiling and singing to herself and doing little dancing steps. She didn't seem to notice Sam at all.

Sam sat absolutely still. She knew without question that the red dress had once belonged to this lovely dancing lady. She knew it the way you often find you know things in dreams — without anyone telling you or explaining anything. She didn't dare to move.

Then a flicker in the corner of her eye made her jerk her head around.

'All right, lass, steady on,' said a voice in the shadows. And out stepped the green-and-black triangle dress. The person in it had wavy pepper-and-salt hair and the sort of determined, cheerful face that made Sam quite sure she was a teacher of some kind. Under her arm she carried a big black purse, and on her feet were sturdy black shoes.

'I'm Miss King,' she said.

'Hello,' said Sam.

Miss King looked across the room at the lady in the red dress, who was now slipping off her shoes and rubbing her feet, as though they were tired. Her shoes were lovely: delicate silver dancing slippers, with straps and slender high heels.

'This is very curious,' said Miss King. 'What am I doing here — all dressed up for school? I've been retired for years. I must be dreaming, I suppose.' She smiled faintly.

'I think I'm dreaming, too,' said Sam, suddenly finding her tongue.

'We can't both be dreaming the same dream, lass,' said Miss King firmly.

'I think the clothes have done it,' Sam said hesitantly. 'I think your dress ... must be a Special.'

'Oh, no, dear.' Miss King looked at Sam with her head a little to one side. 'Nothing special about this. It was a

very useful dress — marvellous really — never showed the dirt. Oh, I wore it to school year in, year out. It became quite an institution, I'm afraid. The littlies used to draw pictures of me standing in front of the blackboard, always wearing this poor old dress. Mind you, it's not bad, even now ...'

'Well, I'm for bed!' rumbled a voice from the chair across the room, and a figure rose up and stretched. Sam blinked against the light. What next!

'Hold on,' muttered the voice. 'Where am I? What's going on? Holy dooley, this is a turn-up for the books!'

An old man in a tartan dressing-gown shuffled towards them. He stared at Miss King and Sam with rather bloodshot, and very surprised, eyes. 'What's the game?' he asked them. 'What's the story?'

'I'm afraid I can't enlighten you,' said Miss King primly. 'I think I'm having a dream.'

'You're having a dream — that's rich!' drawled the old man. 'Here *I* am in some place I've never seen before, wearing me old gown I haven't seen for ages, and you tell me *you're* dreaming.'

He patted the pockets of his gown, and looked disappointed to find them flat and empty. Then he clasped his hands behind his back and looked around the room. 'Funny place, this,' he observed after a while. 'Looks like an old clothes shop, eh?'

'It's my house!' Sam said. 'We've been collecting old clothes for the fete.'

'Is that so?' said the old man, staring around with interest. 'Looks like some good stuff you've got here … Good old stuff.' He turned to Miss King. 'The old fabrics last, eh?' he said. 'This gown now. Real high quality stuff it is — have a feel.' He held out an arm and Miss King gingerly fingered the dressing-gown sleeve.

'Very nice,' she murmured politely.

'I'll say it's nice,' said the old man enthusiastically. 'A real bottler, this old gown. Warm as toast of a winter's evening. Me wife give it to me — years ago. She's gone now, the wife …'

His voice trailed off. Sam felt very sorry for him, but couldn't think of anything to say. He stood with his hands in the pockets of the gown and his head tucked into his chest. Suddenly he spoke again, a bit more cheerfully.

'Funny this old gown turning up again. That's one in the eye for Cynthia — me daughter-in-law, that is. Poor old Cyn, she's a wonderful woman — but that houseproud! Likes everything, you know, just right. Strike me! As soon as I moved in with them she started getting after me about this gown, wanting to give it away. Like a dog with a bone, she was. Wouldn't leave it alone.' He rubbed his nose thoughtfully.

'Y'know,' he said, 'I was sure she *had* give it away to someone or other — got me a new one, anyway, but I never took to it. The old one did me. Would have seen me out, I reckon. Me daughter — she's in New Zealand now, you know — she used to say this gown was like me second skin. She said in a letter once — writes a lovely letter, Margie does — that when she thought about me she always saw me wearing me old gown, sitting in front of the Essie heater back at home with me tobacco in one pocket, and a few Minties in the other, for her and her brother to find. Their mum'd say: 'Kiss yer father, clean yer teeth, and bed!' And they'd come and give us a kiss, and there'd be a Mintie each for them before they done their teeth and popped off to blanket bay.'

He looked down again and Sam caught the twinkle of tears in his eyes. She felt her own eyes prickling. Even Miss King was looking thoughtful.

'Excuse me!' said a soft voice beside her. 'I'm terribly sorry but I'm a bit confused about exactly ...'

'We're all confused, love,' said the old man to the lady in the red dress (for it was she who had spoken). 'Looks like there's been some sort of mix up.

'It must be a mass hallucination,' said Miss King in a determinedly calm tone. 'I've read about such things occurring — in foreign countries, of course, among excitable people — but I never ...'

'Well, I don't know,' said the lady in the red dress doubtfully. 'I suppose it must be something like that. I mean, I suddenly find myself here — wearing this dress, of all things. My Special!'

Sam jumped in her seat.

'The thing I can't understand,' said the lady, 'is that I haven't worn this for — oh, years. I thought I'd given it away to my sister, before we moved to London. I can't understand how I can even fit into it. I was tiny in those days.'

'What days?' asked Sam.

'Oh, I was twenty when Mum bought this for me.'

The three others stared at her. She didn't look more than twenty now! Something funny was going on, that was certain.

'It cost the earth,' said the lady, smiling. 'Heaven knows how poor Mum paid for it, but I never even thought about that then. I wore it to my twenty-first birthday party, and then to a few dances and things. I met my husband at one of them, actually.' She laughed. 'I used to wear Mum's fur with it. I thought I was Christmas! I've never had such a beautiful dress since.'

'Why did you give it away?' said Sam. She thought that if she'd had a dress like that, she'd never have parted with it.

The lady shrugged and pushed back her light brown hair.

'Oh, well,' she said, rather sadly. 'I really didn't have anywhere to wear it. Oh, and I'd gained a bit of weight after the children were born, and it didn't fit any more, and that made me cross. And somehow, though I loved the dress, it reminded me of times I thought were dead and gone.'

She smiled. 'When you're living in a muddle of nappies and porridge and kindergarten talk from morning till

night, that sort of life seems very far away. I just didn't feel like the same person who'd worn that dress any more … You wouldn't understand, little love.'

'I can a bit,' said Sam, who knew that grown-ups had their problems, and also knew all about the toll babies took on well-ordered, peaceful lives. It had been very easy living at home before Toby came along — but then, she had to admit, not nearly so much fun. And of course babies grew up, and things quietened down again. She'd often heard Mum and Dad reminding each other of that.

As if the lady had followed her thoughts, she smiled again.

'Oh, of course, later I was sorry I'd given away the dress. My husband was sorry, too. He says he often thinks of me wearing it. We've got a picture of us dancing at a ball. It was the night we got engaged, and I was wearing the dress. It's only a black-and-white picture, but the children often look at it — it really takes their fancy, for some reason. I suppose it's because their father and I look so happy — and young … not much older than they are now.'

She put her hand up to her forehead. 'This must be a dream, mustn't it?' she said. 'I've been going on and on and no-one's interrupted. I suppose the White Rabbit will tum up any moment now.'

'I wouldn't be a bit surprised,' said Miss King, smiling rather grimly.

'Eh?' grunted the old man, who had been staring at something on the other side of the room. 'Surprising, I'll say! Have a geek at that old bird over there.' He pointed.

4. Mrs Houndstooth

Over in the corner a woman was bent over, rummaging in one of the boxes. She was wearing the houndstooth checked suit. Sam hadn't liked the suit when she'd first seen it, and for some reason liked it even less now, even though all she could see of it was stretched tightly over a very broad bottom.

'She shouldn't be doing that,' she whispered anxiously to Miss King. 'My mother has everything fixed for tomorrow morning. She had to take two days off work to get it all done.'

Miss King cleared her throat. 'Excuse me, madam!'

'Yes?' said the lady in the houndstooth suit, straightening up and turning around. She certainly didn't look very friendly.

'I understand that no-one is supposed to go through this merchandise until tomorrow,' said Miss King.

Sam held her breath.

'Are you in authority here?' snapped the lady.

'I simply know the rules,' said Miss King calmly, 'and I'm pointing them out to you.'

The houndstooth lady laughed. Sam wondered how a person *could* laugh and still look so unpleasant.

'I see. Well, thank you, dear,' said the lady to Miss King. 'I think I'm capable of deciding on my own course of action under those circumstances.' She turned back to her rummaging.

'Don't mess up Mummy's things!' squeaked Sam. 'Stop it!' She ran over and tugged the houndstooth skirt. 'Stop it!' She was nearly in tears.

The lady turned around and glared at Sam. She towered above her, and her eyes were cold and black below thin eyebrows drawn in with black pencil — like a devil in a play.

'You're a very rude, badly brought-up little girl,' she hissed. 'How dare you touch me like that!'

Sam stepped back, her heart pounding.

The lady craned around and rubbed at the bit of skirt Sam had grabbed. 'If you've marked my suit with your grubby little hands I'll ...'

'I'm sure this little girl didn't mean to be rude,' said the soft voice of the lady in the red dress. Sam felt two soft hands settle on her shoulders. Her heart began to slow, and the pain in her throat to ease.

'Who might you be?' sneered the houndstooth lady. 'You seem rather unsuitably dressed for the occasion, if you don't mind my saying so.'

'Well,' said the lady in the red dress, with more spirit than Sam would have expected, 'since none of us seems to have any idea what the occasion is, or why we're here, I don't really see how you can say that! I might just as well say that *you're* unsuitably dressed.'

'I *beg* your pardon!' the houndstooth lady cried. 'This suit is never unsuitable, on any occasion. It's a good quality, well-cut garment — nothing cheap or flashy about it, anyway.' She looked the red dancing dress up and down and the lady facing her flushed — whether with embarrassment or anger, Sam couldn't tell.

'This suit,' boomed Mrs Houndstooth, 'took me to the office, to town, to church, and to many a social gathering, in its time. People often commented on how well it suited me. The girls in the office where I was, ahem, personal assistant to the chief accountant, used to say that it expressed my personality down to the ground ...' She rocked back and forth on her large, well-shod feet and lifted her chin, pressing her shiny scarlet lips together.

'Ah, those girls — silly little things most of them — you had to keep at them all the time to get any proper work out of them. Oh, I had no patience with them! Unable to take any sort of criticism — always bursting into tears for no reason, resigning over nothing at all ...whereas I ... *I* was the mainstay of that company for twenty-five years. When I retired I was given a magnificent send-off — quite magnificent. A tremendous celebration.'

Sam could just imagine how the people in that office must have celebrated when they finally got rid of Mrs Houndstooth. What a dragon she must have been.

'Strangely enough,' the houndstooth lady went on, 'I haven't worn this suit for quite a while. It became a little tight around the ... hips ... and I put it away. I'd really quite forgotten about it. I've been so busy. My charity work has been occupying so much of my attention recently.

'It's a dreadful thing, isn't it,' she said, peering at the lady in the red dress, 'how much selfishness there is in the world. Certainly it's not pleasant, no-one says it's pleasant, dealing with the poor and underprivileged. But someone has to do it. Someone has to tell these people how to manage their lives, and encourage them to pull their socks up. It simply requires a firm hand. And I can be very firm when I like, I don't mind telling you. I simply speak my mind, and I usually find people don't disagree with me. Not after they get to know me, anyway.'

Sam exchanged glances with Miss King, who was looking very serious. She pitied the people to whom Mrs Houndstooth spoke her mind, with all her heart.

'Now,' said Mrs Houndstooth, 'if you don't mind. The light in here is getting very bad, and I'm sure there are a few things in these boxes that I'd be interested in.'

To Sam's horror she began rummaging through the clothes again, discarding things she didn't want by throwing them onto the floor in crumpled heaps.

'Oh, please don't!' cried Sam, the tears welling up in her eyes. But Mrs Houndstooth took no notice.

The room was indeed growing very dim, as the beams from the bird window faded. Now Sam could only see a jerking shape digging deep into a box, and hear the woman's little grunts as she bent and burrowed in the gloom. She could smell the perfume of the lady in the red dress behind her. The lady gave Sam's shoulders a final comforting squeeze. Then there was a rustle, and a clatter, and a clumping, and she felt rather than saw three figures move past her and confront Mrs Houndstooth.

'Please, madam ...' coaxed the lady in the red dress.

'I must ask you, madam ...' said Miss King.

'Get out of that, you poisonous old biddy!' roared the old man in the dressing-gown.

'HOW DARE YOU!' shrieked Mrs Houndstooth, rounding on them in a fury.

The room was spinning. The angry voices rose higher and higher. Sam thought: 'Mum, I must get Mum.' She backed away and sat down, thump! in the armchair. The noise grew louder and louder, the room was full of whirling shapes and shadows. Sam shut her eyes tight, clapped her hands over her ears.

'Mummy!' shouted Sam.

And suddenly, there was silence.

5. Whispers in the Dark

The door burst open. Lizzie swept in, wearing her apron, with Toby under one arm. She switched on the light. Sam screwed up her eyes against the glare.

'Sammy, darling, what's the matter?' Lizzie was hugging her, Toby tugging her hair with a grimy fist.

'Oh, Mum, Mum, she's wrecked your boxes. They tried to stop her, but ...'

'Darling, darling, you've been having a dream. Poor old thing. Come on, Mum'll get you a nice ...'

'No, Mum, no! Look!' cried Sam and pointed ...

'Nothing's wrong, sweet. Everything's OK. You don't have to worry. Look, see?'

And it was true. Everything was back in place. The red dress shimmered on its hanger by the wardrobe, the green-and-black triangles hung primly on a rack. The old dressing-gown slumped against the chair across the room, and the houndstooth checked suit sat, rigidly folded, on the chest of drawers. The boxes stood as tidily as ever — you would never have known they'd been disturbed.

Sam sat staring at it all.

Toby struggled to get down, and Lizzie swung him to the floor. He scampered off on all fours, exclaiming with interest as he poked among the racks.

'Now, come on, my love, and help me finish the pancake mixture. Then you and Toby can have a bath together. Would you like that?'

'Pancakes!' said Sam. 'Yum!' The mysteries of the clothes room seemed suddenly impossible to talk about. They'd disappeared with the shadows when the light went on. She'd think about it all later, talk to Mum and Dad about it later ...

'Ada!' cried Toby. 'Gollygolly, galah, galah.' He poked his head out from behind a box and came wagging up to them, triumphantly dragging something.

'What have you got there, monkey?' said Lizzie. She bent down.

It was a silver shoe. The lady's silver shoe.

'That's funny,' said Lizzie. 'How could I have overlooked this? It must have rolled under the cupboard or something.'

Sam opened her mouth to speak, but changed her mind. It was all too difficult.

'Where's the other one?' wondered Lizzie. She scrabbled around under the wardrobe, and gleefully pulled out the matching shoe.

'How about that, eh, Sam? Aren't they pretty?'

Sam thought they were everything shoes should be. They were as light and delicate and made for dancing as the lady in the red dress had been when she was twenty. And they hadn't been there before. She knew they hadn't.

'They're beautiful!' she breathed.

Lizzie fastened the shoes together by linking their straps, and wrote out a label for them from the supply of blanks on the dressing table.

'Somebody might come at them, do you think, Sam?'

Sam looked at the price and mentally counted up the money in her piggy bank. She sighed to herself. The shoes were beyond her means, anyway.

'Come on, all! Let's go,' said Lizzie. She ushered the children out, switched off the light and shut the door.

Sam wondered if the clothes were whispering in the dark.

6. The Fair Begins

'Well, we're off, Sambo!' said Lizzie.

The first arrivals were walking briskly across the asphalt. Sam, standing between her mother and Mrs Curl under the striped awning with its 'Pre-Loved Clothes' sign, blushed and looked down at her toes as the people approached. She was excited, shy and proud to be behind the scenes at the fete this time, not just an onlooker and visitor. How often she had envied Whitey McGoo, standing behind his huge father who always wore the same apron with 'Kiss the Cook' on it, every year on the hot-dog stand. How pleased she had been last year when Lizzie had worked for an hour on the hoop-la, her tummy big with curled-up, unborn baby Toby, and Dad had helped to put up the stalls.

But this year, they were really *in* it all! They had their own stall, and a cash box of their own, with silver coins sitting snugly in their separate compartments in a tray, and notes folded neatly beneath.

She peeped up to see whether the first customers had arrived at the stall yet. Her eyes widened. They'd walked straight past!

She looked at her mother. Lizzie smiled.

'Don't worry, Sam,' she said. 'We'll be busy enough as the day goes on. Those ladies are the real early birds. They know what they're after, don't they, Lyn?'

'Too right,' grinned Mrs Curl. 'Every year it's the same thing. Those old ducks are in like Flynn, first thing, to snap up Marg Maxwell's sponges and the other goodies from Cakes, and the best of the jams. By the time they're finished there'll be nothing but chocolate crackles and the packet-mix cakes left on Marg's stall, and marmalade on Jams.'

'It's not really fair to the late-comers, is it?' said Lizzie. Naturally, her family was *always* late.

'Oh, well,' said Mrs Curl, with a shrug. 'The idea's to sell the stuff, I suppose. It doesn't matter who buys it, as long as it goes.'

Sam relaxed and let her thoughts wander. And then, quite suddenly, the strange experience of the afternoon before flooded back to her. That strange dream — or whatever it had been — those people. Somehow pancakes, bed and the exciting rush and bustle of fete morning had muffled the memory, dimmed her certainty that it had all really happened. But now she turned and saw Miss King's dress heading a rack on her left. The old man's dressing-gown

hung beside Mrs Curl. The beautiful red dress flirted with the breeze at the very front of the stall, on one of Lizzie's own padded satin hangers, with the silver shoes at its hem. And, with a chill, she saw out of the corner of her eye a flicker of black and white at the top of a box behind her.

There they all were, the Specials (for she knew that this was what they were). But what about the people whose Specials they had been? Where were they now? Would they mind these clothes, that had been part of

them, going to other people?

Now she saw that some customers had drifted up to the stall. They were going through the racks and boxes — and buying. More and more people came. Soon there was a crowd. T-shirts, school blazers, beanies and skirts, jumpers, shorts, dresses and jackets came tumbling over the counter with notes and coins, an avalanche for Lizzie and Mrs Curl to cope with.

Lizzie was laughing and chatting. Her cheeks were red, her nose was shiny. Mrs Curl's hair was shedding its pins and falling down. They stuffed the clothes into bags, passed over the change. The cash box wasn't neat any longer — and it was nearly full. Sam sold a pinafore to a grandma, and a hat with a feather in it to a girl from the house next-door to the school. She was careful with the change, and didn't make any mistakes. She kept an eye on the Specials. So far they were untouched. A few people looked at them, but no-one wanted to buy. The Specials waited, little islands in the chattering, flurrying sea of people and clothes that seethed around the stall.

Then Sam heard a voice she knew. A nice, calm voice.

'Samantha, could I have a look at that green-and-black dress, please?'

It was Miss Wilkinson, one of the Infants' teachers. Sam had always liked her, though some of the kids didn't. She was sometimes a bit strict. On the days Miss Wilkinson was on assembly duty no-one in Infants dared to be late. Just having to creep in and sit at the front of the assembly room under her stern eye was enough punishment to discourage a tendency to linger over breakfast, or chatter in the bag room.

Sam remembered that well. Now that she was older and in Primary she knew that there was nothing to fear about Miss Wilkinson, who was one of the fairest teachers in the school. It had been Miss Wilkinson who found Sam crying and alone after school one day when Dad was late picking her up because the car wouldn't start. Miss Wilkinson had taken her to the office and

given her a drink of water and an Iced Vo-Vo, and had waited with her till Dad came. She hadn't told Dad that Sam had cried.

Sam took down Miss King's dress and gave it to Miss Wilkinson.

'What about this, Mrs Baldwin?' smiled Miss Wilkinson to her friend, the teacher Sam had had in her first year of school. 'Isn't it splendid? So fifties!' She held it up against herself. It suited her, Sam thought.

'Looks in fairly good condition, anyway,' said Mrs Baldwin.

'This would be a really useful dress for school, really useful. Wouldn't show the dirt — wouldn't need much ironing ... I think I'll buy it,' said Miss Wilkinson, rummaging in her purse.

'Oh, come on, Viv — you're not down to wearing second-hand clothes to school, surely,' protested Mrs Baldwin.

'No, I really like this dress. It's friendly. I have a good feeling about it. And it's ... sort of ... suitable. I think I'll get a lot of wear out of it,' insisted Miss Wilkinson. 'Here, Samantha, could you fix this up for me, dear?'

Sam smiled at her. She folded the green-and-black triangle dress carefully and put it gently in a bag. She took Miss Wilkinson's money and proudly gave her the right change. Then she handed her the bag — with the dress that was starting a whole new career. She knew Miss King would have approved.

7. 'Sold'

Mrs Strong bustled up to the stall, cash bag in hand. She counted out the excess notes and coins from the bursting tin, and put them into the bag. 'My word, Second-hand Clothes is doing well this year!' she said, raising her eyebrows. She wrote out a receipt and tucked it under the tray with the notes.

Lizzie beamed. So did Sam and Mrs Curl.

'I'll be back again in an hour, ladies,' said Mrs Strong. 'Barbara is following me with coffee for you.' She strode off briskly in the direction of Jams, swinging the money-bag, satisfyingly plump, against her ample thigh.

The crowd had eased. Lots of people were congregating at the tea bar, where perspiring Mothers' Club members were doling out scones with jam and cream and mugs of tea and coffee. While Lizzie and Mrs Curl drank their coffee and chatted, Sam wandered off with Cecilia Strong to explore the fete.

They had a go at the hoop-la. Cecilia won a little china cat, but Sam missed with all her hoops.

They decided not to have their faces painted.

They bought a hot dog each from Mr McGoo, and said hello to Whitey.

They each had a ride on a rather cranky Shetland pony.

Cecilia bought some paper flowers and a belt made of knotted rope and wooden beads.

Sam bought a mouse bookmark.

They watched a display by the gymnastics club. The human pyramid was very wobbly but stayed up all right, to wild applause.

They each bought a drink with ice in it.

Then Sam had no money left, and she skipped back to the stall. She could see, even from a distance, that lots of things had been sold while she was away. Mrs Strong had been doing her rounds again, and was trotting off towards Jams looking very pleased with herself. And standing in front of the red dress was a slim figure with her hands behind her back. As Sam watched, the figure did a little dancing step. Sam's heart gave a great leap.

Then the figure turned, and Sam relaxed. For a moment she had thought ... but of course this was someone else altogether. A girl with straight brown hair cut in a fringe, wearing jeans and little shiny silver earrings. Her T-shirt had a rainbow on it.

She fumbled in her shoulder bag and found an old brown wallet. Sam watched her as she pulled out a couple of flimsy notes and then started going through her change. Suddenly the girl looked up and saw her. She grinned at Sam in a rather embarrassed way.

'I don't think I can manage it,' she said. She just assumed Sam would know what she was talking about. 'I haven't got enough.'

She turned back to the red dress, the little crumple of money clutched in her hand. Sam came up beside her and looked at it too. The dress flared and shimmered in the sun.

'Would you like to try it on?' It was Lizzie, scenting a sale.

'I don't think I've got ... yes, I would, please,' said the girl. She obviously couldn't resist the chance of wearing the dress, just once, even if the price was too high for her, thought Sam. Sam understood how she felt.

Lizzie took down the dress and ushered the girl into the curtained space she had rigged up as a trying-on room, to Mrs Curl's amusement. Most people didn't bother trying things on, and it had only been used once or twice the whole morning. But Lizzie liked the idea of the changing room, and Sam was glad they had it. It made the stall more like a real shop.

An exclamation penetrated her daydreaming.

'My word!' said Mrs Curl.

Sam looked — and saw a vision in a red dress float out of the ridiculous little cubicle. The dress that was made for dancing had found a new owner. It clung and swayed below a shiny cap of hair, bright young eyes and brown shoulders, fell gracefully to slim tanned feet that side-stepped and posed and side-stepped again.

'Oh, it's superb, it's beautiful!' cried the girl. 'Look, I've absolutely got to have it, but I've only got ...' She rushed back to the cubicle and came back with her little knob of notes and change. She thrust it at Lizzie. 'Look,' she said again, 'could you take this as part payment if I bring the rest this afternoon? I can ...'

'Just a sec,' said Lizzie. She counted the money. 'You aren't much under, and it's getting late. We finish at two. I think ... don't you, Lyn?'

'Oh yes,' said Mrs Curl. 'No question.'

'Oh, are you sure?' beamed the girl in the red dress. 'Oh, thanks. Oh, that's terrific! See, there's a ball, a Uni ball today week, and I … anyway … anyway, isn't it superb?'

Lizzie and Mrs Curl nodded and smiled. Sam found herself nodding and smiling too. They were still nodding and smiling to each other, like idiots, when the girl, ordinary once more in her jeans and T-shirt, had rushed off with a wave and the bulky plastic bag clutched tightly in her hand.

'She didn't ask about the shoes,' said Sam suddenly.

'She didn't need them,' said Lizzie. 'She told me she had some gold ones of her mother's. Anyway, they're sold — to be taken away later — I only left them there for effect.' She turned away and began to tidy the rack behind her.

Sam felt a pang. She looked down at the shoes, still neatly lined up under the place where the red dress had been. Sure enough, they bore a note with 'Sold' scrawled on it in Lizzie's funny writing.

'Who bought them?' she asked anxiously.

'Oh, someone or other, while you were off with Cecilia,' said her mother.

'Excuse me!' snapped someone behind them. 'I presume the stall is still open?'

A lady in green trousers and a frilled blouse frowned at them from the other side of the counter.

'Oh, I'm so sorry,' said Lizzie, hurrying over to her. 'Can I help you?'

'If you *don't* mind my interrupting your conversation,' said the lady, 'I'm interested in this suit. How much is it?'

Sam knew, without looking ... but she looked anyway, and a little shiver ran down her back as the horrible houndstooth snarled at her from between the grasping, plump little fingers with their bright red nails.

'The price should be on it somewhere,' said Lizzie. 'Oh yes, look, there it —'

'Oh, but that's absurd!' said the lady. 'I saw *that*, but I couldn't believe that anyone could really expect such a price. I haven't seen you on this stall before, I don't think. I make a practice of coming every year. My name is Mrs Hall. Agnes Hall.' She waited, as though expecting Lizzie to recognise the name and curtsy or something.

Mrs Curl bustled up. 'Oh, hello, Mrs Hall, how are you?' she said. 'This is Mrs Delaney, who has organised a stall for the first time for us this year. Lizzie, this is Mrs Hall, an old friend of the school's.'

'Yes, my two boys attended school here, in their first years, as it was so handy to our home,' said Mrs Hall loudly. 'Of course, as they got on we had to make other arrangements. I wanted rather more for them than this little school could offer, I'm afraid. They are both exceptionally bright, and I feel that if one can afford the best, one shouldn't hesitate to do the best by one's children.'

'Oh ... certainly,' said Lizzie quietly.

'In any case, I've continued to take an interest in the school, as we do live nearby. And my husband designed the new assembly hall, of course. He gave the school a very good price. Actually, he made practically nothing on the job. But we were pleased, very pleased, to be able to help, to have been in a position to be able to do so. And, of course, I'm still helping.' She gave a booming laugh. 'I find I can make myself useful at parents' and citizens' meetings, when my social obligations allow me to attend. A bit of plain speaking goes a very long way on such occasions, don't you think?'

'Oh … yes …' said Lizzie, looking rather confused.

Sam cringed.

'Now, about the suit, dear,' said Mrs Hall. 'I *thought* the price was a mistake, a result of your inexperience, of course, and I *quite* understand. Organising a stall is by no means the easy matter some young people seem to think. You mustn't be disappointed at your failure this year. No doubt you'll be given another chance next year, perhaps on something a little less ambitious, and then …'

Sam felt herself flush to the roots of her hair. She sprang to her mother's side.

'The stall hasn't been a failure! It's been a terrific success! Mrs Strong says it's the best …'

'It's all right, Sammy,' said Lizzie, gently drawing Sam's pink face into the soft folds of her dress, and stroking her hot cheek. 'Mrs Hall doesn't understand.' She turned back to the indignant woman and spoke to her softly. 'Mrs Hall, naturally I'll be happy to sell you the suit at whatever price you can afford. The stalls are basically to raise money for the school, of course, but if we are able to do anyone in need a good turn along the way, we are very happy to do so.'

Mrs Hall stood gaping while Lizzie refolded the suit and put it in a bag.

'Now, Mrs Hall, just give me whatever you can and we'll say no more about it,' cooed Lizzie, with her sweetest smile.

Agnes Hall had turned a very nasty pinky purple colour. It clashed horribly with her lipstick.

'I assure you, Mrs Delaware, that I am perfectly, *perfectly* capable of paying the full price,' she snapped.

'Mrs Hall,' breathed Lizzie, 'this is just between us. Please don't be too proud to accept a little kindness.'

Something like a moan escaped from Mrs Hall's tight lips. She slammed down a note. 'Keep the change,' she hissed. She grabbed the plastic bag with the suit in it, and made off as fast as she could go, her big green bottom trembling in fury all the way down to the school gate.

'Mum! What happened?' asked Sam, who hadn't quite followed.

'By gosh, you ripper, Lizzie!' Mrs Curl exploded. 'I never thought I'd see the day that one of us'd get Agnes Hall on the run. Bags of money and a heart like a walnut, that woman. What did the old skinflint pay in the end?'

'Only twice the marked price!' said Lizzie smugly. 'Isn't it amazing how it's always the very people who insist other people be grateful for charity that get the most insulted when they're offered charity themselves? I've often noticed it.'

8. The Tartan Gown

The fete was nearly over. Customers were fewer now. Dad arrived with Toby in the stroller, and Lizzie went for a walk with them to get a cup of tea and buy some of the selling-off specials on the Garden stall.

Sam stayed on Lizzie's chair, dreaming. So much had happened over the last couple of days. It would take ages to sort it all out in her mind.

She thought about Miss King, Miss Wilkinson, the lady in the red dress, the girl in the rainbow T-shirt. She thought with a shudder of Mrs Houndstooth and Agnes Hall. She thought about the old man in the dressing-gown ... the old gown still hanging, rather forlornly, it seemed to her now, beside Mrs Curl.

The sun was warm on her face. She smiled to herself and blinked sleepily. Mrs Curl was starting to tidy up. She lifted the old tartan gown down from its hanger, folded it and put it in a box behind the counter. Soon all the unsold clothes would be packed up. Lizzie had said that this year they were going to be given away instead of being stored for next year's fete. She and Mrs Curl agreed that it was a waste for good clothes to be stuck in someone's garage for a whole year when they could be being used. Sam supposed someone would be glad of the old dressing gown. She hoped whoever got it would be nice.

'Hello, Marg,' she heard Mrs Curl say. She looked up and saw Mrs Maxwell from Cakes leaning over the counter.

'I hear Second-hand Clothes did wonderfully well this year,' said Mrs Maxwell.

'Too right,' grinned Mrs Curl. 'The things went like hot cakes — speaking of which, Marg, how did you go? As if I didn't know.'

'Oh, it's always pretty good going on Cakes. Practically all over by ten-thirty, no matter how many we make,' smiled Mrs Maxwell. 'I'm so glad we were back in time for me to do it again this time. I really missed it last year, though if you'd told me that, I'd never have believed it!'

'Hello, Mrs Maxwell,' said Sam, coming over to the counter. 'Where's Fee?'

'Oh, she's coming on with her grandfather and Peter,' said Mrs Maxwell. 'Dad's a bit slow these days.'

'Pretty good, though, isn't he, Marg?' said Mrs Curl.

'Oh, not bad, Lyn. But older. You know,' said Mrs Maxwell. 'He's that tickled to be back living with us

again, though. It didn't work out with Ted and Cynthia. You can imagine ...' She and Mrs Curl exchanged one of those grown-up, not-in-front-of-the-children looks.

Something stirred at the back of Sam's mind. She remembered — Fee and Peter had only come back to school this term. They'd gone away with their parents — something to do with Mr Maxwell's job. Everyone thought it was for good, but then Mr Maxwell was wanted back in the main office, and his company had paid for the family to come back to Australia. Where had they been? She remembered Fee in class, proudly showing them a Maori doll, and a little carved stone she said was called a tiki. Yes, that's right, it was ... New Zealand!

Sam craned her neck around the edge of the stall. Fee and Peter were coming, chattering excitedly as usual. They were walking on either side of a stooping, elderly man in a suit and hat. Each held one of his hands. Every now and then one of them would look up at him and say something, and the old man would nod and smile, and give their hands a little shake. Sam's mouth opened. Her eyes were wide.

'Here we are, then, Margie,' said Mrs Maxwell's father. 'Slow and steady wins the race, eh?' He took off his hat and smiled at Mrs Curl, giving a little bow as he was introduced. Then he saw Sam. A very curious expression came over his face. He stared at her as though he couldn't believe his eyes. Sam stared back, manners forgotten, unable to say a word.

'Sam, this is our Pa,' said Fee.

'I know,' said Sam. 'I knew it would be.'

Fee looked at her.

'I think we've met before, this young lady and me,' said Mrs Maxwell's father.

Sam looked up into the kind, rather red old eyes. A little bit older, a little bit thinner — but it was him all right! She turned around and rummaged.

'Here, Sam, what's up? I've just packed that box. No-one's going to buy any more now, love,' protested Mrs Curl.

Sam's fingers fumbled in the box. Then they found what they were searching for. Flushed, feeling as though she was dreaming, she dragged out the tartan dressing-gown and put it on the counter.

'Well, what'd you know!' said the old man quietly. 'What *do* you know.' He looked first at Sam, then at the gown.

There was a strange little silence.

'Dad! That looks like ... that's ...' gasped Mrs Maxwell.

'Yep. I'd know it anywhere,' said the old man. 'It's me old gown come home to roost. Wonders will never cease!'

'It's incredible,' said Mrs Maxwell. 'Cynthia gave it away, ages ago ... she told me.'

'Maybe it was held over from last year,' said Mrs
Curl. 'Quite a few things were. But Sam, how on
earth ...?'

'Oh, the young lady's a good saleswoman, eh?' said
the old man quickly. 'She could just tell an old bloke like
me'd be a sucker for a comfy gown like this. Isn't that
right, Missie?'

Sam swallowed, and managed to nod. The old man
dipped his head and gave her a wink — so fast that she
blinked, not really knowing if she'd seen it or not.

'What an amazing coincidence, though,' said Mrs
Curl. 'I can't get over it. It was as if she knew ... Sam, how
did ...?'

'Makes a good story, all right,' cut in the old man. 'Anyhow, what's the damage?'

'Oh, no,' said Mrs Curl. 'I can't ask you to pay for your own gown.'

'Look, love, to me it'd be cheap at ten times the price.' He found the ticket on the gown, fumbled in his pocket, and passed some coins over the counter. 'This is my contribution to the fete, eh?'

He turned to Sam. 'Thanks, Missie,' he said, and gave a formal little bow. 'I s'pose at my age you just take miracles in your stride, and you don't ask too many questions. You're just grateful when things pan out. It's a funny old world.' He gathered up the shabby old gown. 'I thought I had everything a man could want when Margie and the kids came home,' he said. 'But now I've really got everything. Me family, and me second skin!'

Sam laughed.

Mrs Curl looked a bit concerned. 'It's very hot in the sun,' she murmured to Mrs Maxwell. 'Maybe your dad should sit down for a while in the shade.'

Margie Maxwell grinned. 'Oh, don't worry about Dad, Lyn,' she said. 'You've just witnessed a very happy reunion, that's all. Funny, though, I can't imagine where he could have met Samantha before ... Dad ...?'

'Come on, Mum,' yelled Fee. 'Dad says come on. He's tooting.'

'Oh, well, see you later, Lyn. 'Bye Sam,' said Mrs Maxwell hurriedly.

'See you Monday, Sam.' Fee darted off, with Peter in tow.

'Bye, Missie,' said the old man. 'Be seeing you, eh?' He nodded to Mrs Curl and walked off with his daughter, holding her arm and clutching the old tartan gown as if it was made of gold.

Sam and Mrs Curl were watching them go as Lizzie slipped back behind the counter.

'Well,' said Mrs Curl, 'that was the strangest thing. Lizzie, you can't imagine the funny thing that happened while you were ...'

'Just hold on a sec, Lyn — sorry I've been so long — Sammy, will you go to Dad at Jams and stand with Toby while Dad gets the car?'

Sam sped off. Her head was spinning.

Toby was sitting in his stroller trying to eat an icecream. Most of it was in his hair. Most of the rest of it was on Old Dog, who had suffered much at Toby's hands in the past and was now going to have yet another adventure in the washing machine on his return home. But some of it had got into Toby's mouth, and he was looking very happy with the experiment.

Sam pushed the stroller to and fro. People wandered across the playground, homeward bound, loaded with pots and parcels, sticky with icecream, sausages, jam and cream, each person looking forward to something different — a cup of tea, a little nap, a quiet read, noisy games in someone's backyard. Lots of separate lives, sometimes crisscrossing, sometimes mingling, sometimes running parallel and never meeting.

'Come on, Sammy,' called Dad. 'Bring the little crook. We're going.'

Sam wheeled Toby to the car, parked by the stall. The stall was bare and lonely-looking now. The leftover boxes were stacked in the back of the car. The changing-room curtain was folded on top. Soon Mr Da Costa and his team would be taking down the stall, for return to the hiring place.

It was all over.

9. Something Special

'Home again, home again, jiggety-jig!' sang Dad. The car bumped along. 'We'll get Chinese take-away for dinner, eh, Liz?'

'I'll say,' sighed Lizzie. 'That'd be great.'

'Went well, I gather?' Dad grinned at her.

'Oh, it went really well. *Double* last year's profit. Just shows what a bit of organisation will do ... oh, heavens, I sound like that ghastly Mrs Hall.' Lizzie laughed.

'Who's ...?'

'Oh, that reminds me, for some reason I can't fathom ...' Lizzie twisted round in her seat to look at Sam. 'Sam, what was Mrs Curl saying about Margie Maxwell's *father's* dressing-gown? I couldn't really understand it.'

'Oh,' said Sam. 'It was his Special, and he found it again. He was very pleased.'

'But, Sam, Lyn said you ...' Lizzie stopped. Sam saw her father glancing at her in the rear vision mirror. She moved uncomfortably in her seat belt.

'It's one of those funny things,' she said, and felt herself flushing. 'It's a bit hard to explain.'

'Oh, well,' said Dad, 'you think about it and then tell us, eh?'

Sam knew she would. Not today, but sometime soon.

All was quiet. Toby lay spreadeagled in his cot, deeply asleep, dreaming baby dreams. Dad sat with his feet up on the veranda rails, a book on his lap. Sam sprawled on

her tummy in her room, doing a jigsaw, eating an apple, and thinking.

Lizzie came in and knelt beside her. 'I'm going to have a sleep, Sam,' she said. 'I'm exhausted.'

'OK, Mum,' said Sam.

'Thank you very much for all your help on the stall, darling,' said Lizzie. 'You were terrific.'

'That's all right. I liked helping. I loved it,' said Sam. 'Can we do it again next year?'

'Well, we'll see,' smiled Lizzie. 'Anyway, I bought you something, as a thank-you present. Funny sort of present, but I thought you might like it.' She brought out a bag from behind her back. Sam took it and peeped inside. There, nestled in tissue paper, lay the silver shoes.

'Oh, Mum!'

'For dress-ups, or whatever,' said Lizzie. 'They just appealed to me. Maybe you'd lend them to me, if I wanted to wear them sometime. They fit me — just!'

'We'll share them. Gee, Mum! Thanks!'

When Lizzie had gone Sam picked up the shoes and put them on the shelf with her cowrie shell, peacock feather, swimming certificate and lucky stone.

One day, perhaps, she'd wear the shoes, really wear them, to dance in, to be grown-up in. But for now they would ornament her treasure shelf, and tell her stories in the late afternoons.

She plumped back onto the floor amid the jigsaw pieces, scattered in her excitement. Suddenly she saw one special piece she had been looking for. She seized it and put it into place, saw another, and another, and gradually the fascinating business of making a picture from fragments drew her in, as it always did.

In the spare room the bluebird window glowed and the sunbeams played. They touched the armchair, patched the faded carpet, flickered in the wardrobe mirror. But all was peace, and no whisperings disturbed the silent air.

Emily Rodda's first book, *Something Special*, was published with Angus and Robertson in 1984. It marked the beginning of a career that has seen her become one of the most successful, prolific and versatile writers in Australia.

Since then, Emily has written or co-authored over ninety books for children. Her children's books range from picture books to YA novels, and include the award-winning Rowan of Rin series as well as the outstandingly successful Deltora Quest fantasy series.

A full-time writer since 1994, Emily has won the Children's Book Council of Australia's Book of the Year Award a record five times and seems to instinctively know what children want to read.

A NEW STORY FROM INTERNATIONALLY
RENOWNED CHILDREN'S AUTHOR
EMILY RODDA

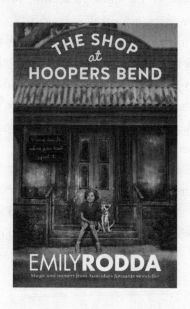

When Quil Medway gets on the train, she thinks she knows where and how her journey will end. At camp. With another school holiday spent surrounded by people, but feeling alone.

Quil doesn't know how wrong she is. She doesn't know anything about the shop at Hoopers Bend.

Or a bitter, prickly woman called Bailey. Or a little black and white dog who at this very moment is chewing through a rope so he'll be free to answer a call that only he can hear.

She doesn't know about the magic. But it won't be long now …

From one of Australia's most renowned children's authors, this is a story about coming home — when you didn't even know that was where you belonged.

'I wish something would happen!' said Rachel. 'Something interesting!'

Afterwards, she would remember what she'd said and how she'd felt, that rainy Saturday morning, and she would think, 'That was really the beginning,' and her stomach would give a little jolt.

But at the time she didn't know what was in store. All she knew was that she was bored. Bored with having a cold and staying in bed. Bored with the rain drumming on the roof. If only something unexpected would happen for a change.

Something exciting — something wonderful.

'Maybe it will!' her father said, 'And pigs might fly!'

But he was only teasing. Pigs can't fly — can they?

A children's fantasy favourite for over thirty years, *Pigs Might Fly* was Emily Rodda's second book and won the prestigious Children's Book Council of Australia's Book of the Year for Younger Readers Award in 1987.

Cecilia says merry-go-rounds are for little kids, but Jo feels there's something mysterious and not at all childish about the carousel that has appeared overnight in Marley Street.

There's something odd about the beckoning music; something strange about the gleaming horses. And why are some people allowed to buy tickets to ride while others are turned away?

Jo wants a ticket. She wants it badly.

But will she be riding into danger?

A children's fantasy favourite for over thirty years, *The Best-Kept Secret* was Emily Rodda's third book and won the prestigious Children's Book Council of Australia's Book of the Year for Younger Readers Award in 1989.